A. Beasty Bites

B. Jungle Java

C. Savanna Library

D. House of Bones

E. Amazon Security

F. Everyday School

G. Wild'n'Wooly Barber Shop

H. Arctic House Post Office

I. Monkey Bowl

J. Porpoise Pool

K. Big Cat Toys

L. Gator Grocery

Boyd

Arnold

Coach Pouch

Harley

Hayley

The Umpire

This book is dedicated to my grandson Chase,
whose smile lights up an entire room.
—J. M.

To Jessie and Edgar
—M.S.

ZONDERKIDZ

Field of Peace
Copyright © 2012 by Joyce Meyer
Illustrations © 2012 by Zondervan

Requests for information should be addressed to:

Zonderkidz, 5300 Patterson Ave SE, Grand Rapids, Michigan 49530

ISBN: 978-0-310-72318-9

Scriptures taken from the Holy Bible, *New International Reader's Version*®, NIrV®. Copyright© 1995, 1996, 1998 by Biblica, Inc.™ Used by permission of Zondervan. All rights reserved worldwide.

Joyce Meyer is represented by Thomas J. Winters of Winters, King & Associates, Inc., Tulsa, Oklahoma.

Zonderkidz is a trademark of Zondervan.

Illustrator: Mary Sullivan
Contributors: Jill Gorey, Nancy Haller
Editor: Barbara Herndon
Art direction and design: Cindy Davis

Printed in China

13 14 15 /LPC/ 10 9 8 7 6 5 4 3 2

Let the peace of Christ rule in your hearts …

Colossians 3:15

EVERYDAY ZOO

JOYCE MEYER
Field of
Peace

pictures by **MARY SULLIVAN**

ZONDERkidz

ZONDERVAN.com/
AUTHOR**TRACKER**
follow your favorite authors

Everyday Zoo was buzzing with excitement. It was baseball season, and the Wilds were on their way to winning the championship.

"Watch out, Gabby! Here … comes … my … CRAZY BALL!" Boyd shouted from the pitcher's mound. Then he swung his arm wildly and the ball zig-zagged through the air toward Gabriella Goose.

The umpire yelled, "Steee-rike three!"
"Great game!" Arnold Armadillo shouted.
"We win again!" Boyd cheered, as he did a little victory dance.
"Thank you, God, for a great game!"

The next day, Boyd's picture was in the newspaper.

"Winning the championship would be the most AWESOME thing in the entire world!" Boyd said. "I've waited my whole life for this!"
"But you're only seven," Harley reminded him.
Boyd couldn't wait to win that trophy.

The players took their places on the field. Boyd
stood on the mound, and every time he pitched the ball,

it zigged ... and zagged ...

and zoomed through the air—striking out each batter.

Arnold cheered, "Way to go, Crazy-Ball Boyd!"

It was another exciting game, and the Wilds were ahead, until it was Arnold's turn at bat.

Arnold marched up to the plate.

Just as he was about to swing, a bumblebee landed on his nose.

Arnold wiggled and jiggled and jumped all around trying to get it off.

And instead of Arnold hitting the ball ... the ball hit Arnold.

"Where did Arnold go?" Harley asked Coach Pouch.

"Right there," Coach said, pointing to a large, bumpy-looking ball sitting next to home plate. "That's how armadillos protect themselves when they're scared."

And for the rest of the game, whenever the ball got too close...

"I got it!"

"I got it!"

"He didn't get it."

For the first time that season, the Wilds lost a game.

Arnold felt terrible. Boyd felt worse. He really wanted to win that trophy.

Coach patted Arnold on the back. "Don't worry," he said. "The next game will be better."

But it wasn't. The same thing happened ... again and again.

"It's okay. You can come out now, Arnold. The game is over."

"Arnold's going to ruin our chances of winning the championship," Boyd grumbled, as he stormed off the field.

The next day, Boyd showed up early for the final game, accidentally startling the new groundskeeper.

When Coach arrived, he decided to move the game to Critter's Field.
"Boyd, can you stay and let the rest of the team know where we're playing?"
"Sure, Coach," Boyd said, covering his nose.

As the players arrived, Boyd told them to go to Critter's Field and checked their names off his list. Finally, the only name left was Arnold's.

"If he doesn't show up soon, I'll be late," Boyd grumbled.

 −  =

As Boyd stood there waiting, he started to imagine what would happen if Arnold didn't show up at all...

Boyd really wanted to win that trophy. So he ignored the sinking feeling in his stomach, and left without telling Arnold the game was moving to Critter's Field.

EVERYDAY ZOO
COMMUNITY FIELD
HOME GUEST
0 0 0 0

The championship game was underway at Critter's Field, and Boyd was feeling worse than ever. In fact, his insides were zig-zagging more than his crazy ball.

Every time he looked at the baseball,
all he could see was Arnold's face staring
back at him.

Coach called a time-out and gathered the team together.
"Without Arnold, we seem to have lost our spirit," he said.
"I miss him," said Hayley. "I wonder why he didn't come."

Boyd was afraid to tell his friends the truth, but he couldn't keep his secret any longer.

"Because I didn't tell him the game moved to Critter's Field!" Boyd confessed. "I thought we might have a better shot at the championship without him."

"But it wouldn't be much fun to win without Arnold," said Harley.

Coach put his arm around Boyd. "When we make good decisions that please God, we feel calm and peaceful inside. Do you feel peaceful about leaving Arnold behind?"

"NO!" Boyd said. "I do NOT feel peaceful! I feel ABSOLUTELY POSITIVELY AWFUL!"

"You know how the umpire makes all the important decisions in a ball game?" said Coach. "Well, I know a great umpire that will help you make good decisions in life. That umpire's name is PEACE."

"But where does peace come from?" Hayley asked.

"It doesn't come from winning, having trophies, or being in the newspaper," Coach said.

"It comes from doing things that make God happy!" Boyd shouted as he ran off the field.

"Where are you going?" Harley called after him.

"TO GET ARNOLD!"

It was the final inning, and the Wilds were behind when Arnold nervously stepped up to the plate. The bases were loaded, and his team *had* to score.

Once again, as the baseball came whizzing in his direction,
Arnold got scared and rolled into a ball.
But this time, as he dropped the bat, he heard a small *crack*.

ARNOLD HIT THE BALL!

As the crowd in the stands cheered, Boyd yelled, **"Roll, Arnold, roll!"**

And that's just what Arnold did. He rolled as fast as he could around the bases—first, second, third...all the way back to home plate.

"Safe!"

The Wilds won the game!

Boyd felt very good about winning the trophy. But even better than that...

...he felt peaceful.